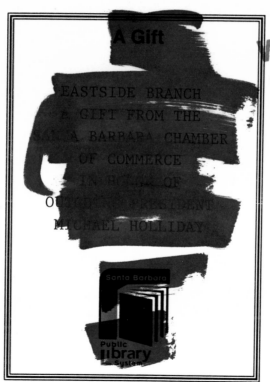

W9-CUI-228

MEET THE NURSE/
TE PRESENTO A LOS ENFERMEROS

By Joyce Jeffries

Traducción al español: Eduardo Alamán

Gareth Stevens
Publishing

Please visit our website, www.garethstevens.com. For a free color catalog of all our high-quality books, call toll free 1-800-542-2595 or fax 1-877-542-2596.

Library of Congress Cataloging-in-Publication Data

Jeffries, Joyce.
[Meet the nurse. Spanish & English]
Meet the nurse = Te presento a los enfermeros / Joyce Jeffries.
     p. cm. — (People around town)
ISBN 978-1-4339-7388-8 (lib. bdg.)
1. Nurses—Juvenile literature. 2. Nursing—Juvenile literature. I. Title. II. Title: Te presento a los enfermeros.
RT61.5.J4413 2013
610.73—dc23

                                                    2012012856

First Edition

Published in 2013 by
Gareth Stevens Publishing
111 East 14th Street, Suite 349
New York, NY 10003

Copyright © 2013 Gareth Stevens Publishing

Editor: Katie Kawa
Designer: Andrea Davison-Bartolotta
Spanish Translation: Eduardo Alamán

Photo credits: Cover, p. 7 Creatas/Thinkstock; p. 1 michaeljung/Shutterstock.com; pp. 5, 13, 21, 24 (bandages, scrubs) Hemera/Thinkstock; pp. 9, 24 (scale) Jose Luis Pelaez/Iconica/Getty Images; pp. 11, 15 iStockphoto/Thinkstock; p. 17 Lisa F. Young/Shutterstock.com; p. 19 Brian Eichorn/Shutterstock.com; p. 23 Washington Post/Getty Images.

Printed in the United States of America

CPSIA compliance information: Batch #CS12GS: For further information contact Gareth Stevens, New York, New York at 1-800-542-2595.

Contents

What Do Nurses Do?. .4

In a Hospital 10

Kinds of Nurses .16

Words to Know .24

Index. 24

Contenido

¿Qué hacen los enfermeros?. 4

En un hospital .10

Tipos de enfermeros. 16

Palabras que debes saber 24

Índice 24

Nurses help us
stay healthy.

Los enfermeros nos
ayudan a mantenernos
sanos.

They can work in groups. These are called teams.

Los enfermeros pueden trabajar en grupo. Estos grupos se llaman equipos.

A nurse sees how much
a person weighs.
She uses a scale.

La enfermera pesa
a una persona. La
enfermera usa una
báscula.

Some nurses work
in a hospital.
They help sick people.

Algunas enfermeras
trabajan en el hospital.
Ayudan a las personas
enfermas.

They wear special clothes. These are called scrubs.

Los enfermeros usan ropa especial. Es el uniforme de enfermería.

They write on charts.

Las enfermeras escriben
la historia médica.

Some help very old
people. They work
in a nursing home.

Algunos enfermeros
trabajan en hogares
de ancianos. Ayudan
a las personas de edad
avanzada.

Some work in schools.

Algunos enfermeros
trabajan en las
escuelas.

19

They cover cuts.
They use bandages.

Los enfermeros curan
heridas. Los enfermeros
usan vendas.

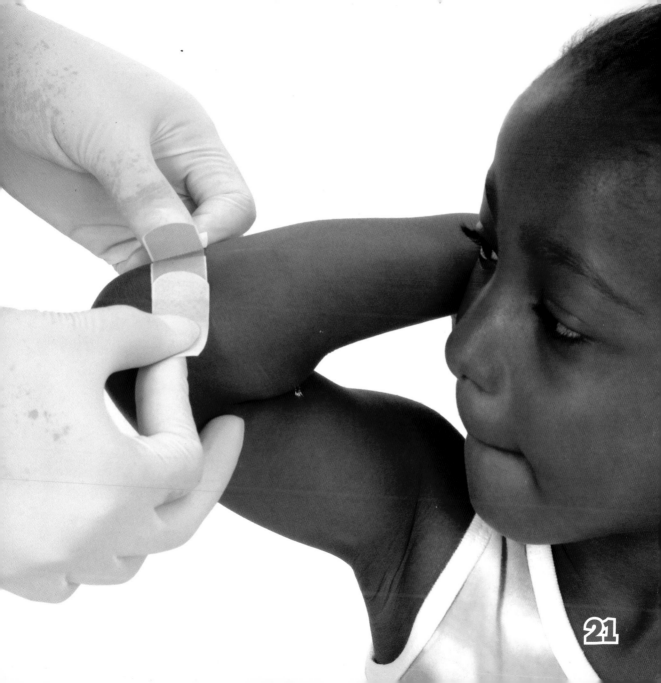

21

Some work on planes!
These are flight nurses.

¡Algunos enfermeros
trabajan en aviones!
Estos son enfermeros
de vuelo.

Words to Know/ Palabras que debes saber

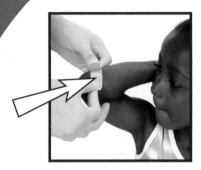

bandage/
(la) venda

scale/
(la) báscula

scrubs/
(el) uniforme
de enfermería

Index / Índice

hospital/(el) hospital
10

schools/(las) escuelas
18

nursing home/(el) hogar
de ancianos 16

teams/(los) equipos 6

24